LOST IN THE JOURNEY OF MAGIC

MIR MARIAM

Contents

Dedication

Allah, the Most Merciful and Benevolent, who has blessed me with the gift of life, the power of imagination, and the ability to write. I am eternally grateful for guidance, wisdom, and unwavering support of Allah.

My parents, Mohamad Muzzafer Mir and Ursilla Taranum, who have been my constant source of love, encouragement, and strength. Your selfless devotion and unwavering belief in me have shaped me into the person I am today. I am forever grateful for your sacrifices and prayers.

And especially to my dear sister, Mir Maham, who has been my rock, my confidante, and my inspiration throughout this journey. Your kindness, patience, and generosity have meant the world to me. Your presence in my life is a blessing from Allah, and I cherish every moment we share.

Thanks to Allah, for blessing me with such an amazing family. Thank you, Mom and Dad, for being my pillars of strength. And thank you, dear sister, for being my partner in every sense of the word. This book is a testament of your love, support, and encouragement."

Foreword

"Get ready to embark on a thrilling adventure with Leo and Zoe, two siblings from New York who find themselves transported to a magical world of wonder and discovery. As they navigate this strange and fantastical realm, they'll encounter incredible challenges that will test their courage, creativity, and unity.

But as they face their fears and doubts, they'll learn the power of positive thinking and the strength that comes from believing in themselves. With every step, they'll discover the boundless potential of their own imagination and the unbreakable bond of sibling love.

Through their journey, "Lost in the Journey of Magic" explores timeless themes of hope, resilience, and the transformative power of unity. With its richly imagined world, memorable characters, and inspiring message, this enchanting tale will captivate readers of all ages and leave them with a renewed sense of wonder and awe.

So join Leo and Zoe on their epic quest to find their way home, and discover the magic that lies within yourself."

Preface

"Welcome to 'Lost in the Journey of Magic,' a tale that has been woven from the threads of my imagination and inspired by the love and support of my family.

I am Mir Mariam, a 12-year-old student from Achabal, and I am thrilled to share my debut book with you. Born to Mohamad Muzzafer Mir and Ursilla Taranum, I have been encouraged to chase my dreams and explore my creativity from a young age. My parents' unwavering support has been the wind beneath my wings, and I am forever grateful to them. And also I want to express my gratitude to my sister Mir Maham for always encouraging me and helping me write this book. I started my educational journey at Smart Kids Digital Play School, currently attend Saint Xain's International School in 7th class. In recent years, I have been fascinated by the world of English literature. My passion for reading and writing has grown exponentially, and I am proud to call myself an avid reader. My journey as an Aloha student has also played a significant role in shaping my writing skills and nurturing my love for the language.

This book is a reflection of my imagination, creativity, and dedication. This story has been brewing in my mind for a long time, and I am excited to finally share it with the world.

I hope that 'Lost in the Journey of Magic' will transport you to a world of wonder, inspire you to chase your dreams, and remind you that magic can be found in the most unexpected places.

Thank you for joining me on this enchanting journey. I hope you will enjoy the ride!"

Acknowledgements

"I am forever grateful to the people and experiences that have made this novel possible.

First and foremost, I thank Allah, the Almighty, for blessing me with the gift of writing, the power of imagination, and the opportunity to share my story with the world. This novel will be a reflection of your beauty and a testament to your greatness.

To my family, that has been my rock, my inspiration, and my guiding light: thank you for your unwavering support, love, encouragement and your belief that meant the world to me.

To my parents, Mohamad Muzzafer Mir, and Ursilla Taranum who instilled in me a love for stories and imagination: thank you for your sacrifices, patience, and guidance. Your influence has shaped me into the person I am today.

To my dear sister, Mir Maham who has been my partner in every sense of the word: thank you for your kindness, generosity, and unwavering support. Your presence in my life is a blessing from Allah.

To my friends, mentors, and fellow writers who have offered valuable feedback, encouragement, and inspiration: thank you for your time, expertise, and camaraderie.

And to the readers, who have joined Leo and Zoe on their magical journey: thank you for embracing their story and making it your own.

This novel is a testament to the power of love, family, imagination, and faith. I hope it has touched your heart and inspired your spirit."

Prologue

"Imagine a world where dreams and reality blend together. A world of wonder, magic, and endless possibility.

In a small corner of New York, two siblings, Leo and Zoe, are living ordinary lives. But little do they know, their lives are about to take an extraordinary turn.

As the moon shines down on the city, a gentle breeze whispers secrets of the past. It's a call to adventure, a summons to explore the unknown.

Leo and Zoe are about to discover a world beyond their wildest dreams. A world of enchantment, danger, and discovery. Join them on a journey that will test their courage, imagination, and the bond between them."

LOST IN THE JOURNEY OF MAGIC

Characters:

Mom

Dad

Leo

Zoe

1

Lost in the reflections of the Ice

Once upon a time, in the bustling city of New York, two siblings, Leo and Zoe, lived with their parents. One lazy Sunday evening, as they were engrossed in TV, their Mom called out, "Children, come help me clean the storage room! You've spent all day watching TV; it's time to lend a hand!" The siblings reluctantly got up and headed to the storage room, filled with boxes and forgotten treasures.

Zoe stumbled upon an unusual mirror, which she picked up and examined with a curious eye. However, she soon deemed it useless and carelessly tossed it aside. Leo, fascinated by the mirror's intricate design, retrieved it and tucked it into his backpack.

That night, as everyone slumbered, Leo crept into Zoe's room, mirror in hand, eager to share his discovery. Zoe, still half asleep, pushed the mirror away, annoyed. But before Leo could even flip the light switch, the mirror began to radiate a soft, ethereal glow. The siblings were transfixed, unable to speak.

Leo cautiously picked up the mirror, and they both gazed into its mystical depths. To their astonishment, a vibrant, otherworldly landscape unfolded before their eyes. Before they could comprehend what was happening, they were sucked into the mirror's realm, leaving their familiar world.

As they emerged from the mirror's portal, Leo and Zoe found themselves standing on a frozen lake, surrounded by towering ice sculptures that refracted the light in dazzling patterns. The air was crisp and cold, and the silence was almost palpable.

Suddenly, a figure appeared in the distance, gliding effortlessly across the ice. As they drew closer, Leo and Zoe saw that it was a woman with long, flowing hair and a gown that shimmered like the ice itself. Her eyes seemed to hold a deep wisdom, but also a hint of sorrow.

"Welcome, travellers now that you have come you have to find the way to get out of this world," she said, her voice was like a gentle breeze. "I am the Guardian of the Ice. You have entered this realm uninvited but you have to get out before you stuck here forever, and before you ask the 10 days of here is one night of the Earth, but since you are here in the first phase of this dangerous world, you must play by the rules of the mirror."

"What rules?" Leo asked, his curiosity piqued.

"The rules of reflection," the Guardian replied, her gaze piercing. "Every action, every thought, will be reflected back at you. Be careful what you wish for, and be prepared to face the consequences."

With that, she vanished, leaving Leo and Zoe to navigate the treacherous landscape of the ice, where every step could lead to wonder or danger.

Slowly they began to see the reflection of themselves in the ice some showed them as monsters and some showed like other creatures but they glanced the look at a big wall of ice where there was a waterfall with a door behind it, when they saw it the ice shattered and they were in front of the waterfall they went to open the door but it needed a key.

Leo and Zoe stood before the ancient door, their hearts racing with excitement and a hint of fear. The Guardian's words echoed in their minds: "Every action, every thought, will be reflected back at you." They knew they had to find the key to unlock the door, but where would they find it?

As they searched the frozen landscape, they noticed something peculiar. The ice sculptures around them began to change, reflecting their thoughts and desires. A nearby sculpture transformed into a magnificent dragon, its scales shimmering in the light, as Leo imagined himself as a brave warrior. Meanwhile, Zoe's thoughts conjured a beautiful unicorn, its horn shining with a soft, rainbow glow.

"This is incredible!" Leo exclaimed. "Our thoughts are shaping the ice!"

"But how do we find the key?" Zoe asked, her brow furrowed in concern.

Suddenly, a whispery voice spoke in their minds, "The key lies within the reflections of your hearts. Look closely, and you shall find it."

Leo and Zoe gazed into the ice, and as they did, they saw visions of their past, their memories, and their deepest desires. They saw Moments of kindness, courage, and love, and they realized that the key was hidden within their own hearts.

Without a word, they reached out and grasped each other's hands. As they did, their heart's reflections began to merge, creating a brilliant light that illuminated the ice. The light took the shape of a glowing key, suspended in the air before them.

Together, they reached out and grasped the key, feeling its warmth and energy coursing through their veins. With a triumphant cry, they inserted the key into the ancient lock and turned it. The door creaked open, revealing a radiant world beyond the ice.

2

Warming up for Danger

<hr>

When they opened the door an invisible force pushed them in closing the door. There lied a desert with an intense hot temperature. Leo said oh so simply it is the journey from the fridge to the oven. Zoe said shut up! Be serious, we have to get back. They walked a few kilometres, now they were thirsty and wanted water.

Suddenly they caught sight of a traveller. They thought to approach him.

As they drew closer to the mysterious traveller, Leo and Zoe's thirst and exhaustion got the better of them. They eagerly approached the stranger, hoping for water and guidance.

"Please, sir," Leo asked, his voice parched and weak, "can you spare some water?"

The traveller slowly turned to face them, revealing a withered, ancient face with sunken eyes. A cold, mirthless smile spread across their face.

"Water, you say?" the traveller croaked, their voice like the rustling of dry leaves. "I have water, but it comes at a price."

Zoe's instincts screamed warning, but Leo, desperate for relief, nodded eagerly. The traveller handed them a water skin, and they drank greedily, feeling the cool liquid soothe their parched throats.

But as they handed the water skin back, the traveller's smile grew wider, and their eyes gleamed with malevolence.

"You should not have come here," they hissed, their voice like a snake slithering through the sand. "Now, you will never leave."

As the siblings watched in horror, the traveller raised their hands, and the sand around them began to swirl and churn. A massive sandworm erupted from the ground, its jaws wide open, ready to attack them.

Leo and Zoe spun around, sand flying beneath their feet as they sprinted away from the monstrous sandworm. Its jaws snapped mere inches behind them, the sound echoing through the desert like a crack of thunder.

They raced across the dunes, their legs pumping furiously, but the sandworm kept pace, its body undulating through the sand like a living wave. The siblings' breath came in ragged gasps, their hearts racing with fear.

With a final burst of energy, they reached the rocks and scrambled up, their hands and feet finding holds in the rough stone. They collapsed onto a narrow ledge, panting and trembling with exhaustion.

The sandworm coiled below, its eyes fixed on them with an unblinking stare, waiting for them to make another move.

As they caught their breath, they realized that the traveller was nowhere to be seen, but a small, intricately carved stone lay on the ledge beside them, etched with a single word: "Run."

As they caught their breath, they noticed a strange glow emanating from the stone. It began to pulse, and the air around them started to distort. Suddenly, a spectral image materialized before them - a wise, ancient being with eyes that burned like stars.

"You have entered the realm of the mirror's reflections," the being said, its voice like a gentle breeze. "But to escape, you must first confront the shadows within."

With that, the being vanished, leaving behind a small, ornate box. The box opened with a soft creak, revealing a dark mirror that seemed to pull them in. Suddenly there appeared a creature in front of them.

Leo and Zoe exchanged a nervous glance.

As they gazed deeper, visions began to materialize within the creature's depths. They saw fragments of their past, Moments of fear and doubt, and the shadows that lurked within their own hearts.

Leo saw himself as a young boy, afraid of the dark, and the monster that lurked in his closet. Zoe saw herself as a teenager, struggling with self-doubt, and the fear of not being good enough.

The visions shifted, and they saw each other's fears and doubts, their deepest insecurities laid bare. They realized that the mirror was showing them the shadows they had been trying to hide from each other.

Suddenly, the visions merged, and they saw a new image - a combined shadow, a monstrous creature with their collective fears and doubts.

The mirror shattered, and the creature emerged, its presence palpable. Leo and Zoe stood frozen, facing the embodiment of their darkest fears.

The creature, a twisted amalgamation of their deepest fears, lunged at them with a deafening roar. Its razor-sharp claws swiped through the air, barely missing Leo's face as he dodged to the side. Zoe tried to run, but the creature's tail ensnared her, pulling her back into its grasp.

Leo leapt forward, determined to save his sister. He grabbed a nearby rock and slammed it into the creature's jaw, momentarily stunning it. Zoe took advantage of the reprieve, using her agility to wriggle free from the creature's tail. Together, they said we are not afraid of you we know you are just blackmailing us emotionally. While saying this Leo observed a handle on the wall he understood it was a hidden door whispered in his sister's ears about the door. They thought of a plan Leo just distracted the creature while she opened the door and they just ran away and closed the door with all their strength.

3

Facing the Echoes

Leo and Zoe stood at the entrance of the maze, its twisting paths and mirrored walls seeming to stretch on forever. Reflection's voice whispered in their minds, "Face your echoes, and you shall find the way out."

As they ventured deeper, the mirrors began to echo their memories, whispers of their past mistakes and fears. Leo saw himself as a young boy, struggling to protect Zoe from their father's anger. Zoe saw herself as a teenager, doubting her own worth and beauty.

The echoes grew louder, more insistent, until they became a cacophony of self-doubt and fear. But Leo and Zoe knew they had to push forward, facing their inner demons. But Zoe said why there is only self-doubt everywhere. Leo said because it is the only thing to make a person weak. Zoe gazed at him, having tears in her eyes because now she knew that her brother was by her side.

As they navigated the maze, the echoes grew louder, more insistent. Leo and Zoe knew they had to confront their inner demons head-on.

Suddenly, a figure emerged from the shadows. It was their father, his eyes blazing with anger and disappointment.

"You're just like your mother," he sneered at Zoe. "Weak and useless."

Leo felt a surge of anger, but he knew he had to stay calm. "That's not true," he said, his voice firm. "Zoe is strong and capable. And we're not afraid of you." And Zoe it is just an illusion, don't trust in them.

Their father snarled, his face twisted in rage. But Leo and Zoe stood firm, facing their echoes with courage and determination.

As they did, the mirrors began to shatter, one by one. The echoes faded away, replaced by a warm, golden light.

"Well done," Reflection's voice whispered in their minds. "You have faced your echoes and overcome them. Now, find the door with the golden handle, and you shall escape the maze."

They were searching for the golden handle but it was nowhere; it was just an empty hall where their voices echoed. Suddenly Leo said wait we can say positive things they would also echo. Zoe said OK. They started to say positive things which gave them confidence. Suddenly she found the golden handle. She was about to open it when Leo jumped in and said I will open this one please I just want to and Zoe agreed.

4

The Time Trap

Leo and Zoe found themselves standing in a sleek, dark chamber, surrounded by gleaming metal walls and a web of pulsing blue lines. A holographic display flickered to life before them, projecting an imposing figure with a stern expression.

"Welcome, adventurers," the figure declared. "You have entered the Time Trap, a challenge designed to test your unity and ingenuity. You have 60 minutes to complete three tasks. Failure will result in... Consequences."

The display vanished, and a countdown timer appeared on the wall, ticking away with ominous intensity.

Task 1: The Maze of Reflections

A section of the wall slid open, revealing a labyrinthine mirror maze. The reflections of Leo and Zoe stared back at them from every angle, creating a dizzying illusion.

"You must navigate the maze together, using your combined wits to overcome the illusions and reach the centre," a voice instructed.

With each step, their reflections multiplied, making it harder to distinguish reality from illusion. But Leo and Zoe moved in perfect sync, using their knowledge of each other's strengths and weaknesses to overcome the challenges.

Task 2: The Harmony of Elements

A large, circular platform emerged from the floor, divided into four sections representing earth, air, fire, and water. A melodic voice guided them:

"Create harmony among the elements by solving the puzzles etched into each section. You have 20 minutes."

Leo and Zoe divided the tasks, using their unique skills to solve the puzzles. Zoe's knowledge of ancient cultures helped decipher the earth section, while Leo's understanding of physics unlocked the secrets of air and fire. The water section required their combined efforts, as they used their knowledge of astronomy to align celestial bodies and unlock the final puzzle.

Task 3: The Cipher of Unity

A holographic display materialized before them, displaying a complex cipher.

"Decode the message using your collective knowledge and experience," the voice instructed. "You have 10 minutes."

Leo and Zoe pooled their knowledge, using their experiences and insights to decipher the code. With each passing Moment, the solution became clearer, until finally, they entered the correct sequence, and the cipher dissolved.

The countdown timer stopped at 0:01.

The chamber erupted in a celebration of lights and sounds, and the imposing figure reappeared, a hint of a smile on his face.

"Well done, adventurers! Your unity and determination have overcome the impossible. You have proven that together, you can achieve greatness."

As the Time Trap dissolved, Leo and Zoe shared a triumphant glance, their bond stronger than ever.

5

The Dreamcatcher's Journey

As they passed the time trap they were now in a forest. They were very confused. So they just decided to go with the flow.

As they ventured deeper into the forest, the trees grew taller and the silence more profound. Leo and Zoe walked hand in hand, their footsteps quiet on the soft earth. They had been walking for hours, but the scenery remained unchanged, as if they were trapped in a never-ending loop. Suddenly, a faint humming noise began to vibrate through the air, like the quiet buzzing of a harp string. The siblings exchanged a curious glance and followed the sound.

It led them to a clearing, where a magnificent dreamcatcher hung suspended from a branch. The web was intricately woven, with threads of silver and gold that shimmered like starlight. In the centre, a small crystal glimmered, pulsing with an ethereal energy. A figure sat cross-legged beneath the dreamcatcher, shrouded in a hooded cloak that seemed to blend with the shadows.

"Welcome, travellers," the figure spoke in a low, melodious voice. "I have been expecting you. You seek the

Dreamstone, but first, you must face the dreams that haunt you.

The dreamcatcher's web began to glow, and the crystal at its centre pulsed with an intense light. Leo and Zoe felt a strange sensation, as if their minds were being drawn into the web. Visions began to flicker before their eyes, like fragments of forgotten memories.

Leo saw himself lost in a dark forest, chased by shadowy creatures that seemed to embody his deepest fears. Zoe saw herself standing on a precipice, staring into an abyss that seemed to symbolize her own self-doubt.

The dreamcatcher spoke again, "Face your fears, and you shall find the strength to overcome them."

As the visions faded, the siblings looked at each other, knowing they had to confront their inner demons. They took a deep breath and stepped forward, into the heart of the dreamcatcher's web.

The world around them dissolved, and they found themselves in a realm where their deepest fears and desires took shape. They knew they had to navigate this surreal landscape to reach the Dreamstone and unlock the secrets of the mirror.

Leo and Zoe ventured deeper into the dream realm, where their subconscious minds created twisted landscapes and creatures that tested their courage. They encountered manifestations of their own self-doubt, fear of failure, and anxiety, but they refused to back down.

In a desert of shattered mirrors, they confronted the fragments of their own broken dreams and reassembled the shards into a radiant mosaic of hope.

In a labyrinth of whispering shadows, they silenced the voices of fear and doubt by speaking their truth and affirming their bond.

As they navigated the surreal terrain, the siblings discovered hidden strengths and unlocked the secrets of their own hearts. They realized that their unity and determination were the keys to overcoming any obstacle.

Finally, they reached the Dreamstone, a glittering crystal that pulsed with the power of their collective dreams. As they grasped it, the dream realm dissolved, and they found themselves back in the forest, facing the dreamcatcher.

"Well done, travellers," the dreamcatcher said, its voice like a gentle breeze. "You have faced your fears and unlocked the power of your dreams. The Dreamstone will guide you on your journey, but remember, the greatest strength lies in your bond with each other."

With that, the dreamcatcher vanished, leaving Leo and Zoe to continue their quest, armed with the power of their collective dreams and the unbreakable bond between them.

6
Lost in the Jungle

In the blink of their eye, the place was completely different. The portal's radiance dissipated, revealing a vast, underground chamber. The ceiling disappeared into darkness, and the walls were lined with glittering crystals that refracted the light in dazzling patterns. The air was cool and still, filled with the scent of damp earth and hidden secrets.

Leo and Zoe stood at the edge of a tranquil lake, its waters reflecting the crystal hues like a mirror. The silence was almost palpable, broken only by the soft lapping of the water against the shore. As they explored the chamber, they stumbled upon ancient ruins, covered in mysterious symbols and markings that seemed to hold secrets of their own.

Suddenly, they heard a faint whispering in their ears, a soft, melodic voice that seemed to come from all around them. "Welcome, travellers," it said. "You have entered the Heart of the Earth. Here, the secrets of the past await you. Are you ready to uncover them?

As they touched the first tablet, the symbols burst into a vibrant light, and the whispering in their ears became a clear, resonant voice. "The secrets of the Heart of the Earth are revealed to those who seek wisdom," it declared.

The tablet's surface began to shift, revealing a hidden compartment. Inside, a small, leather-bound book lay waiting. The cover was adorned with strange markings that seemed to shimmer in the light.

Leo and Zoe exchanged a thrilled glance. They opened the book, and its pages revealed ancient knowledge, hidden for centuries. The secrets of the earth's creation, the mysteries of the universe, and the whispers of the forest were all contained within.

As they delved deeper into the book, they discovered a hidden message, written in a code that only the most curious and clever minds could decipher. The message read:

"Where shadows dance, light reveals the path".

Seek the reflection of the heart's desire,

In the depths of the lake, a secret lies in wait."

Leo and Zoe pondered the enigmatic message, their minds raced with possibilities. They knew they had to uncover the meaning behind the cryptic words. After a Moment of contemplation, they decided to explore the lake's depths, searching for a connection between the message and the mysterious body of water.

They carefully made their way around the lake's edge, noticing that the crystals embedded in the walls seemed to be pulsing in harmony with the whispering voice. The air was filled with an electric anticipation, as if the very atmosphere was urging them to uncover the secrets hidden beneath the surface.

As they reached the lake's centre, they spotted a glimmering light emanating from beneath the water. Without hesitation, they dove into the lake, the cool liquid enveloping them like a silky shroud. The light grew brighter, guiding them deeper into the depths.

Suddenly, they found themselves in a vast underwater chamber, the walls adorned with glittering gemstones that refracted the light into dazzling patterns. In the centre of the chamber, a magnificent crystal statue rose from the floor, its facets reflecting the light in a kaleidoscope of colors.

The statue depicted a figure with outstretched arms, as if embracing the universe. The siblings approached the statue, feeling an energy emanating from it, as if it held the secrets they sought. As they reached out to touch the crystal, the whispering voice spoke once more, its tone filled with an otherworldly wisdom:

"The reflection of the heart's desire lies within.

Seek the truth in the depths of your own soul."

Leo and Zoe gazed into each other's eyes, understanding that the journey was not just about uncovering secrets but also about discovering their own hearts' desires. They knew that they had to continue exploring, not just the mysteries of the lake, but also the depths of their own souls.

And so, their journey continued, a never-ending quest to uncover the secrets of the Heart of the Earth, and the secrets of their own hearts...

7
The Quest Continues

The angel's words echoed in their minds as they stood there, wondering what lay ahead. "Unity" was the power Leo possessed, but what about Zoe? What was her special gift?

Before they could ponder further, a mysterious mirror appeared, and a figure within it spoke, "I was lost in this challenge, now I am trapped in the mirror's... you have to get out." The figure vanished, leaving the mirror to taunt them, "You've come this far, huh? Okay, so let me tell you that in this dangerous stage, you have to face... nothing." With a puff of dust, the mirror disintegrated, leaving behind only silence.

Leo threw up his hands, "Why do they always confuse us?" Zoe's giggle had long faded, replaced by a determined look. She stepped forward, her eyes scanning the empty space where the mirror once stood. "I think I understand," she said, her voice filled with a newfound conviction. "We've been relying on external clues and guidance, but now it's time to trust ourselves. We need to face our own fears, doubts, and limitations. That's what the mirror meant by 'nothing'."

Leo's eyes widened as he grasped her meaning. "You're right, Zoe! We've been given the power to overcome our own inner demons. Unity and... Self-discovery?"

With a shared nod, they took a deep breath and stepped forward, ready to face the unknown challenges that lay ahead. The quest continued, and they were determined to see it through to the end.

As they ventured deeper, the air grew thick with an eerie silence. No whispers, no echoes, just an unsettling stillness. They walked for what felt like hours, the darkness seeming to swallow them whole. Suddenly, they found themselves standing in a vast, empty space.

"Look!" Leo whispered, his voice barely audible. "Nothing."

Zoe's eyes scanned the horizon, and she nodded. "The mirror was right. We have to face nothing."

The emptiness stretched out before them like an endless canvas, devoid of any shape, form, or sound. Leo and Zoe exchanged a nervous glance.

"Well," Leo said, taking a deep breath, "I guess we just... wait?"

Zoe closed her eyes, her face serene. "We need to embrace the void. Let go of our fears and expectations."

As they stood there, the silence began to feel almost palpable, like a physical presence wrapping around them. It was as if they were being asked to confront the very essence of nothingness itself.

Time lost all meaning as they stood there, suspended in the void. It was as if the universe had paused, waiting for them to make a move. Leo's mind raced with thoughts, but he couldn't grasp any of them. Zoe's eyes remained closed, her face a mask of calm.

Suddenly, a faint hum whispered through the silence. It grew louder, becoming a gentle vibration that resonated through every cell of their bodies. The air began to shimmer, like the surface of a pond on a summer's day.

A low, soothing voice spoke, echoing off the emptiness. "You have faced the unknown, and the unknown has faced you. Now, you must face yourselves."

As the voice faded, the vibration ceased, and the shimmering air settled. Leo and Zoe opened their eyes to find two figures standing before them. The figures were identical to themselves, mirroring their every move.

"Who are you" Leo asked, his voice barely above a whisper.

The mirror-Leo smiled. "We are the reflections of your true selves. The parts of you that you've hidden, denied, or forgotten."

Zoe's mirror-image spoke, her voice a gentle echo of Zoe's own. "You must confront and embrace us, for we hold the keys to your true potential."

Leo and Zoe exchanged a hesitant glance, then nodded in unison. They knew they had to confront their mirror-reflections, no matter how daunting it seemed.

The mirror-Leo spoke, his voice a perfect replica of Leo's own. "I am the part of you that fears failure that doubts your abilities. You've hidden me away, but I've been guiding your actions, holding you back."

Leo's eyes narrowed. "I won't let you hold me back anymore."

With a newfound determination, Leo reached out and embraced his mirror-reflection. As they merged, a surge of energy coursed through his body, and he felt a weight lift off his shoulders.

Zoe's mirror-image smiled. "I am the part of you that's been hurt, that's afraid to trust. You've locked me away, but I've been whispering your deepest fears."

Zoe's eyes welled up with tears. "I won't let you control me anymore."

With a gentle touch, Zoe embraced her mirror-reflection. As they merged, a warm light enveloped her, and she felt a sense of peace wash over her.

The mirror-reflections dissolved, leaving Leo and Zoe feeling lighter, freer. They looked at each other, and their eyes locked in a newfound understanding.

"We did it," Leo said, his voice filled with wonder.

Zoe nodded, a soft smile on her face. "We faced ourselves, and we're stronger because of it."

As they stood there, the emptiness around them began to fill with a soft, golden light. The light grew brighter, and they felt themselves being lifted off the ground.

"We're rising," Leo whispered, his voice full of awe.

Zoe's eyes shone with tears. "We're rising above ourselves."

And with that, they vanished into the light, leaving the void behind. We have also completed this stage Leo said .Zoe annoyed told that when is it going to end I am tired. Leo said we should rest for a while here. Saying this they laid down to sleep without knowing that the net stage is the most dangerous.

8

The adventurous field

They were in deep sleep as they were really tired but they felt some movement, to their surprise when they opened their eyes they were caught by the tribal people of the jungle. Zoe was so scared that she screamed which even made Leo awake. Suddenly a voice came from the sky, you have been caught by the kazi tribal people how silly of you to sleep in the forest now let's see how you will escape this chapter of this world. Leo said oh no we have to do something. Zoe struggling to get her hands off the stick which was held by ropes said that we have to cut the rope. Leo said how on earth will you do that, oh I remembered you have really sharp teeth, when you bit me when we were fighting I wore bandage for a whole week so I guess. No stop joking around as she was about to decide anything they saw the tribal people litting the fire up. Zoe said in a low voice do they eat humans, Leo said yes like I was reading an article about tribal people. Zoe interrupted stop we have to find a way out of here.

She suddenly remembered my necklace which Mom gave me on my birthday. It is pretty sharp to cut these ropes I guess, Leo said no are you in your senses how your necklace can cut the rope. After some silent movements of thinking Leo said ouch, something is pinching me in my shoe, he somehow managed to get the shoe out he saw that a piece of mirror was there. Yes Zoe said we will cut the ropes with this shattered piece of mirror. They freed themselves from the ropes and ran as fast as they could, suddenly Leo said everything there is a door but this time it isn't a door Zoe took a glance at the back saw the key in the neck of the head of the tribe, she told Leo about it Leo said I guess this time there is magic a magical door yes we have to take that key.

Leo said yes I have an idea, before he could ever share his idea they heard a loud scream. They ran and saw the tribe was being defeated and people of that tribe were getting killed by the others, they were just about to hurt the leader when Leo and Zoe jumped in and started to fight with the opposite tribe named karkota tribe. They obviously didn't have the power to fight like them , but they had the power of thinking very cautiously , they made a strategy when the karkota tribe were about to beat them they would come in the front of other members of karkota tribe so that they could just slip away and their other members would get hurt.

After a lot of bloodshed, the kazi tribe won. The tribe head looked towards them and without uttering a word he gave them the key and suddenly a magical golden door appeared before them. Then the head of the tribe said you deserve to get off this ugly world , you were given a task you could have just let us die then take the key but with your wisdom you understood that karkota means demon . They were the evil tribe. He said that you do not choose violence you are something different , you are peacemakers , have a happy journey ahead and yes don't panic. I will remember you in my prayers . They welcomed them by a very warm smile. Saying this they inserted the key and opened the door.

9

Lost in the mystery city

They emerged into the most beautiful city ever, they were surprised by its beauty. But there were no people, but they didn't seem to be much bothered. They found an apartment with food and a bed to sleep in. They were so hungry like they haven't eaten in years but to their surprise even one day didn't end. They were having pain in their legs and arms because of the tight ropes wrapped around their limbs. They found some oil and massaged themselves, then they watched TV for some time like they used to in their own world, they remembered their time they spent with their parents watching movies. Then they finally got themselves tucked in the bed. They were in a very sound sleep when suddenly they were awakened by a frightening voice, and to their surprise it was a tornado.

To escape they took some food and ran away from the tornado as fast as they could and somehow managed to escape from it. Before even processing what happened to them they glanced a look towards the sky which was looking ready to pour a lot of rain. They took some raw materials and made a cabin-like structure to stay in because they were exhausted, then it started to rain. When the rain stopped, they went out and Zoe slipped and fell into a hole. Leo was scared but he wanted to help her sister so he also went in the hole.

There was a fairy waiting for him , she told him this chapter was all about seeing their love for each other and he took the dangerous step to come in this dark hole to save your sister , you two are truly amazing here is the key . They took the key and ran towards the door in the cave.

10
Beyond the Mystic Mountains

With the key in hand, Leo and Zoe embarked on a perilous journey beyond the Mystic Mountains. The fairy's words echoed in their minds, "You two are truly amazing." But they knew that their greatest challenge lay ahead.

As they ventured deeper into the mountains, the path grew treacherous and steep. They encountered raging rivers, treacherous cliffs, and hidden crevices. But with their combined strength and determination, they overcame each obstacle.

The air grew thinner and the winds howled around them, but they pressed on, their hearts pounding with excitement and fear. They discovered hidden caves, ancient ruins, and mysterious artefacts, each one leading them closer to their destiny.

Suddenly, a fierce storm struck, threatening to engulf them. But they pressed on, their hearts pounding with excitement and fear. And then, a magnificent creature emerged from the stormy skies. Its body shone like gold in the lightning flashes, and its eyes burned with an inner fire.

Leo and Zoe gasped in unison, awestruck by the creature's beauty and power. "You have been chosen for a great purpose," it spoke in a voice that echoed in their minds. "Your journey will be fraught with danger and wonder. But know that you are not alone. You have each other, and together, you will face whatever lies ahead."

With that, the creature vanished as suddenly as it had appeared, leaving Leo and Zoe staring at each other in wonder. They knew that their journey was far from over, and that the greatest challenges and wonders still lay ahead.

They continued on, their journey taking them through enchanted forests, across scorching deserts, and over treacherous seas. They encountered fierce dragons, cunning wizards, and mysterious sorceresses, each one testing their courage and wit.

But through it all, they stood together, their bond growing stronger with each passing day. And finally, after many long and arduous months, they reached the threshold of a hidden world - the Realm of the Elements.

The elemental guardians, powerful beings of earth, air, water, and fire, awaited them. "Prove your worth, adventurers," they declared. "Unlock the Elemental Core, and claim your place among the legends of old."

Leo and Zoe accepted the challenge, ready to face whatever lay ahead, as long as they had each other. And with that, they stepped forward, into the unknown, their hearts filled with wonder and excitement.

11

The Elemental Core Unleashed

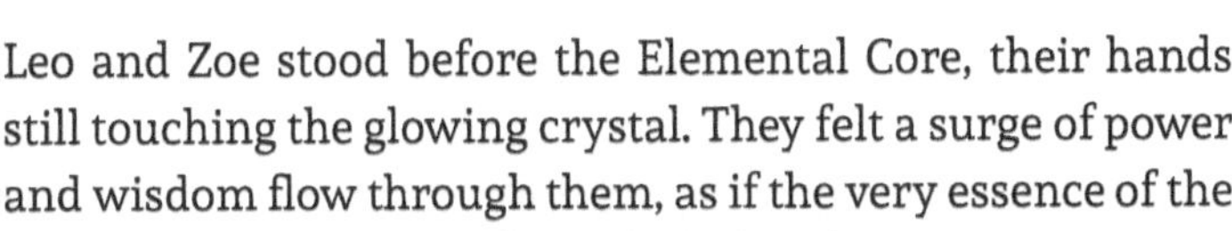

Leo and Zoe stood before the Elemental Core, their hands still touching the glowing crystal. They felt a surge of power and wisdom flow through them, as if the very essence of the elements was coursing through their veins.

Suddenly, the Core began to glow even brighter, and the air around them started to shimmer and distort. The Elemental Guardians stepped forward, their eyes shining with a fierce intensity.

"The Elemental Core has chosen you," the Earth Guardian declared. "You have unlocked its secrets and harnessed its power. Now, you must use this power to restore balance to the Realm."

As she spoke, the ground began to shake and tremble. The skies grew dark, and a fierce wind began to howl. The Elemental Core was unleashing its power, and Leo and Zoe were the only ones who could control it.

They raised their hands, and a blast of energy shot out, striking the ground with a deafening crash. The earth trembled and shook, and the skies grew darker still. But then, a brilliant light began to shine, illuminating the darkened landscape.

The Elemental Core was unleashing its full fury, and Leo and Zoe were harnessing its power. They stood tall, their hands raised high, as the elements raged around them.

And then, in an instant, it was over. The earth stopped shaking, the skies cleared, and the wind died down. The Elemental Core's power had been unleashed, and balance had been restored to the Realm.

Leo and Zoe stood panting, their hands still raised high. They knew that they had truly become something legendary, something that would be remembered for generations to come.

The Elemental Guardians approached them, their eyes shining with respect and admiration. "You have done what was thought impossible," the Water Guardian said. "You have unlocked the secrets of the Elemental Core and restored balance to the Realm." They got a key which was made of ice by the Guardian of ice they opened the door.

12

The Dark Sorcerer's Revenge

When they opened the door they went inside, they stood victorious, basking in the glow of the Elemental Core. But their celebration was short-lived, as a dark figure emerged from the shadows.

"You may have restored balance to the Realm," the sorcerer sneered, "but you have also unleashed a power that will be your downfall."

The sorcerer raised his hand, and a dark energy shot towards Leo and Zoe. But they were ready. They combined their powers, using the elements to create a powerful shield.

The dark energy hit the shield with a loud crash, but Leo and Zoe held firm. They then counterattacked, unleashing a blast of energy that sent the sorcerer flying across the room.

As the sorcerer struggled to get up, Leo and Zoe approached him. "We won't let you harm us or the Realm," Leo declared.

The sorcerer snarled, but Leo and Zoe were unmoved. They used their powers to bind him with chains of earth and air, rendering him powerless.

"You may have underestimated us," Zoe said, "but we are the chosen ones of the Elemental Core. And we will always defend the Realm."

With the sorcerer defeated, Leo and Zoe turned to the Elemental Guardians. "We did it," Leo said, grinning. "We saved ourselves and the Realm."

The Guardians smiled, their eyes shining with pride. "You have truly become something legendary," the Water Guardian said. "Your names will be remembered for generations to come."

And with that, Leo and Zoe walked away from the sorcerer, ready to face whatever adventures lay ahead. For they knew that they were strong enough to overcome any challenge, as long as they had each other.

13

The Whispering Woods

Leo and Zoe ventured deeper into the Whispering Woods, their senses heightened as they navigated the treacherous terrain. The trees seemed to close in around them, their branches creaking ominously in the wind. The air was thick with an otherworldly energy, and they could feel the weight of the woods' secrets pressing down upon them.

Suddenly, a faint whispering echoed through the forest, the words indistinguishable but the urgency clear. Leo and Zoe exchanged a glance, their hearts racing with anticipation.

As they walked, the whispering grew louder, the words becoming clear. "Turn back now, while you still can." But Leo and Zoe were not ones to shy away from a challenge. They pressed on, their hearts pounding with excitement and fear.

The woods grew denser, the trees twisting and turning in ways that seemed impossible. The whispering grew louder, more urgent, but Leo and Zoe pushed on. They could feel the magic of the woods pulsing through their veins, drawing them closer to the secrets they sought.

Finally, after what seemed like hours of walking, they saw it. A massive stone door, adorned with strange symbols and markings. The Door of Secrets.

Leo and Zoe approached the door, their hearts racing with anticipation. They knew that this was what they had been searching for. The secrets of the woods, the secrets of ancient magic.

But as they reached out to touch the door, it swung open, revealing a dark and mysterious passageway. Leo and Zoe exchanged a nervous glance. They knew that they had to go through with it. They took a deep breath and stepped forward, into the unknown.

The passageway was narrow and winding, the walls lined with ancient stones. The air was thick with dust and the scent of old magic. Leo and Zoe walked in silence, their hearts pounding with excitement and fear.

As they walked, the passageway began to slope downward, leading them deeper into the earth. The air grew colder, the darkness pressing in around them. But Leo and Zoe pressed on, their hearts fixed on the secrets that lay ahead.

And then, suddenly, they saw it. A massive underground chamber, filled with ancient artefacts and strange devices. The secrets of the woods, the secrets of ancient magic.

Leo and Zoe approached the chamber, their hearts racing with excitement. They knew that they had finally found what they were looking for. The secrets of the Whispering Woods.

As they entered the chamber, they saw a figure standing in the shadows. It was the Guardian of the Woods, her eyes gleaming with a knowing light.

"Welcome, Leo and Zoe," she said, her voice low and mysterious. "I have been waiting for you. You have proven yourselves worthy by making it this far."

Leo and Zoe exchanged a glance, their hearts pounding with excitement.

"The secrets of the woods are not for the faint of heart," the Guardian continued. "But I sense that you are ready. Come, let me show you the secrets of ancient magic."

She led them deeper into the chamber, showing them strange devices and ancient artefacts. Leo and Zoe listened in awe as the Guardian explained the secrets of the woods.

As they reached the heart of the chamber, the Guardian stopped before a massive stone pedestal. On top of the pedestal lay a small, glowing crystal.

"This is the Heart of the Woods," the Guardian said, her eyes gleaming with reverence. "It holds the power of ancient magic. With this crystal, you will be able to unlock the secrets of the woods and wield the power of the magic."

Leo and Zoe gazed at the crystal in awe, their hearts pounding with excitement. They knew that this was what they had been searching for.

But as they reached out to take the crystal, the Guardian's eyes flashed with a warning. "Remember, the power of magic comes with a great cost. Use it wisely."

And with that, she vanished, leaving Leo and Zoe alone in the chamber. They looked at each other, their hearts racing with excitement and fear. They knew that their adventure was far from over.

Leo and Zoe gazed at the crystal in awe, their hearts pounding with excitement. They knew that this was what they had been searching for.

With trembling hands, they reached out and took the crystal. As soon as they did, the chamber began to shake and tremble. The walls began to close in on them, and the air grew thick with an otherworldly energy.

Leo and Zoe knew that they had to get out of there, fast. They turned and ran, the crystal clutched in their hands. They could hear the Guardian's voice behind them, warning them of the power of the magic.

They emerged from the chamber, gasping for air. They looked at each other, their eyes shining with excitement and fear.

They knew that their adventure was over, but they also knew that their lives would never be the same. They had unlocked the secrets of the Whispering Woods, and they had the power of the ancient magic at their fingertips.

And with that, they vanished into the woods, ready to face whatever lay ahead. They got a wooden key this time and they opened the door.

14

The Road Ahead

They came inside and were thinking what to do but they walked away from the woods, their hearts still racing from their adventure. They had uncovered the secrets of the mysterious woods, and their lives would never be the same.

As they emerged from the trees, they felt a sense of uncertainty. What lay ahead? Would they find answers or more questions? They had solved the mystery of the woods, but they knew that their journey was far from over.

They looked at each other, their eyes locking in a silent understanding. They knew that they would face whatever came next together. They had been through so much already, and they were ready for whatever lay ahead.

Leo took a deep breath, his eyes scanning the horizon. "What's next?" he asked, his voice barely above a whisper.

Zoe shrugged, her eyes fixed on the distance. "I don't know," she said, "but I'm ready to find out."

They walked on, their footsteps echoing in the stillness. The sun was setting, casting a golden glow over the landscape. They walked in silence, their minds processing everything they had been through.

As they walked, the landscape around them changed. The trees grew taller and the sky grew darker. Leo and Zoe could feel a strange energy building up inside them, an energy that they couldn't explain.

But they didn't need to explain it. They knew that they were on the threshold of a great adventure, an adventure that would change their lives forever.

They walked for hours, the darkness growing thicker around them. They didn't need a map or a compass. They knew that they were heading towards something new, something exciting.

And finally, after what seemed like an eternity, they saw it. A light in the distance, shining like a beacon in the darkness.

Leo and Zoe exchanged a glance, their hearts pounding with excitement. They knew that their journey was far from over, but they were ready for whatever lay ahead.

With a sense of determination, they walked towards the light, ready to face whatever came ahead.

Leo and Zoe walked towards the light, their hearts filled with a sense of wonder and excitement. As they drew closer, they saw that it was a road, stretching out into the distance.

"This is it," Leo said, his voice barely above a whisper. "This is the road ahead."

Zoe nodded, her eyes fixed on the horizon. "We've been through so much already," she said. "But I know that this is just the beginning."

Leo took a deep breath, feeling a sense of determination rise up inside him. "We're ready for whatever comes next," he said. "We're ready to face whatever lies ahead."

Together, they took their first steps onto the road, feeling a sense of adventure and possibility stretch out before them. They knew that the journey ahead would be long and difficult, but they were ready to face it together.

As they walked, the light grew brighter, illuminating the path ahead. They knew that they would encounter challenges and obstacles along the way, but they were ready to overcome them.

The road ahead was uncertain, but one thing was clear: Leo and Zoe were ready to face it together, side by side.

And with that, they disappeared into the horizon, ready to face whatever lay ahead. The road stretched out before them, a path filled with promise and uncertainty. But one thing was certain: Leo and Zoe were ready to face it together, their bond stronger than ever.

As the sun dipped below the horizon, casting a golden glow over the landscape, Leo and Zoe walked on, their footsteps echoing in the stillness. They knew that their journey was far from over, but they were ready for whatever came next.

And so, they walked on, into the unknown, side by side, their hearts filled with hope and determination. Thus time they didn't got a key they were confused when suddenly the ground below them disappeared and they were lo and behold in an Ocean.

15

The Journey Back Home

They emerged into a deep ocean. They thought they would be deadin a few seconds but they noticed that they could breathe in the water. They were of course astonished, and a voice came that said, "You have to escape this Ocean. They were ready but before they could even start a shark came and started to chase after them with his sharp teeth looking ready to tear off their flesh. They were scared so they swam as fast as they could, they saw a ship and went inside it. The shark was trying to break in but it was all in vain. They didn't know what to do, and lo and behold Zoe saw a skeleton floating in the water. She was not scared because she knew that it was a skeleton of a person who came here just like them but failed. Leo who was confident was now scared, they were just clueless waiting for any hint or something to help them. They went into a room which was dark and nothing was visible. Their Zoe pushed something which made the ship start and it started to work. They were going ahead as Zoe saw an old box in the ocean , she told Leo but they were unable to stop the ship so they just jumped out of the ship .

They opened the box which was filled with gold and diamonds and a key , they were astonished because there was no door but on the seafloor there was a door which they opened and they were in a room which was surrounded by a pink and white gas and a box having a key in it as they took that key they saw that that were in their room , they thought it was another chapter but they saw a letter on the floor they picked it said ' you became successful in getting out if this world which no one else did and it said to demolish this world which killed thousands of people they kept the key somewhere but you have to figure where ' Leo saw a lock type something behind the mirror Zoe inserted the key in it and the mirror vanished . They did not believe they were in their own world when suddenly their Mom came. You are awake and go to sleep. When their Mom left they hugged each other saying we made it back home. They found a letter saying you were the first travellers to escape this dangerous world. You really are something different.

After that they lived happily and always remained united but didn't forget about this memorable adventure of their life.

And Real Life Begins

ᑭᑭᑭ